THE
WISEST MAN
IN THE
WORLD

A Legend of Ancient Israel

Retold by Benjamin Elkin

Pictures by Anita Lobel

Parents' Magazine Press

New York

For "Reubie the Great"

In days of old, so it is said, a little bee strayed into the palace of the great King Solomon. The angry servants ran to trap it. But the bee escaped from them and flew to the King for safety.

Now this King was the wisest man in the world. So wise was he that he spoke the language of every living thing: of beasts and of fowl, of creeping things and of fishes.

"Mercy, O King," pleaded the bee. "Spare me today, that I may live to serve you tomorrow."

King Solomon smiled to think that this tiny creature could ever hope to serve a mighty monarch. But he drew the curtain and gently released the bee with his own hand. "Go in peace," he said. "I require no service in return."

Through the open curtain the King saw a great caravan. There were hundreds of camels bedecked in gold. There were apes and peacocks, and lions and tigers on jeweled leashes. And at the head of the caravan rode the proud and beautiful Queen of Sheba.

The Queen and her councilors had traveled for many weeks over the vast desert to visit the King.

King Solomon had long been expecting these visitors. He sent a group of nobles to escort them into the palace.

Dressed in his royal robes, the King seated himself upon his throne. Now this was a most wondrous throne, indeed. It was of ivory, covered with gold and precious jewels. Overhead was a golden candlestick with seven branches on each side. All around, hanging crystals flashed their rainbow colors and tinkled like heavenly harps. And most marvelous of all were the two golden lions and two golden eagles which stood on either side of the six steps leading up to the throne. For these golden lions and eagles would permit no one to lie to the King. If anyone dared to tell an untruth, the lions would roar and the eagles would scream.

When the Queen of Sheba entered she could not hide her surprise at King Solomon's splendor. "May the King live forever," she said. "I come to offer you the true friendship of my country."

At once, the golden lions roared and the eagles screamed. For the Queen of Sheba spoke falsely; she had not come as a true friend. But knowing naught of these lions and eagles, the Queen graciously bowed. To her ears, this was another royal salute. In truth, she had long been jealous of King Solomon's fame. And in this visit she hoped to shame him before his own people and before the whole world.

During the next few days the Queen of Sheba did her best to prove that her host was not really wise. She tested his wisdom with difficult riddles. But all of them he readily answered.

Once the Queen brought to him a large diamond which had a curved, twisting hole. "Is it within your power to draw a thread through a winding hole?" she asked.

King Solomon only smiled and sent for a silkworm. The worm crawled through the hole, drawing a thread of silk right through it.

Another time, the Queen sent in sixty little boys and girls, all dressed alike. "If it please Your Majesty," she said, "tell me from your throne which are the boys and which the girls."

To his servants King Solomon said, "Place a basin of water before

each of the children and bid them wash their faces."

Then the boys splashed water on their faces while the girls daintily dabbed the water with their fingertips. And so the King could easily tell them apart.

Once the King and Queen saw that a little dog had fallen into a deep pool. The water was so low that the dog could not be reached. King Solomon tossed a branch into the water for the dog to cling to.

"I would not have done so," said the Queen. "It is better to drown speedily than to starve slowly." And she and her councilors were happy that the King had at last done something so unwise.

But King Solomon did not stop to reply. He showed his men how to block the nearby stream with rocks. As the stream overflowed into the pool, the water rose higher and higher. Soon the branch floated up within reach, and the dog was safely lifted out.

That night the Queen of Sheba met with her councilors. "Thus far we have had no success," she said, "and tomorrow will be our final chance. The King has invited guests from many lands

to a banquet in my honor. For this banquet we *must* find a trick
which will show them that King Solomon is not wise, but a fool."

"Such a trick have we found, Your Majesty," said the councilors.

From King Solomon's garden the councilors plucked a flower. They ordered their craftsmen to make ninety-nine false flowers exactly like it. And then they placed just one fresh flower among the ninety-nine false ones. The copies were so perfect that the Queen of Sheba herself could not point out the real one.

"Well done," said the Queen. "King Solomon will surely pick a false flower as coming fresh from his own garden. By tonight he will be a joke among all the nations."

A gardener heard this and reported it to the King.

But King Solomon had become so proud and confident
that he refused to be concerned. "It matters not," he said.
"It suits me well that they should prove my wisdom before

the multitude, and I fear not what they may do.”

That night the palace gleamed with light as hundreds of
guests came to honor King Solomon and the Queen of Sheba.

At just the right moment the Queen said, "Your gracious Majesty. Our craftsmen beg that you judge their work. Among these flowers only one comes from your garden. The others have been created by my servants in your honor. Won't you select your own flower and let my servants know how theirs compare?"

At first the King was confident of his ability to choose. But when he sniffed the flowers they were all equally fragrant. He felt them, and they were all petal smooth. In beautiful color and appearance, they were identical.

Perhaps this was a trick, and *all* the flowers were false. Then he would be wrong no matter which one he selected.

Never had King Solomon believed that he could thus be entrapped before the guests. As he stood there, puzzled, the guests began to whisper.

What was wrong? Couldn't the King even pick out his own flower from his own garden? Perhaps he was not so wise after all! Even the loyal servants became nervous. Why did not the King make his choice and stop this foolish whispering among the guests?

Then King Solomon felt something tickle his hand. A little bee had landed there. "I am at your service, Your Majesty," whispered the bee. It circled low over the flowers. Then it crawled into the one flower which had honey inside.

No one else had seen the little bee. King Solomon leaned over and plucked out the one flower with the bee in it; the one flower which had grown in his garden.

"Yes," said the King, "your craftsmen are indeed skilled. I have been admiring their work. But the false cannot be true. The others are false, and this one is true."

The Queen checked for the craftsmen's secret mark and then bowed low. Truly, this was the single genuine flower. As the audience applauded, the Queen was finally convinced.

The very next day, the Queen of Sheba and her councilors signed a treaty of friendship with King Solomon.

They left for home, bearing many rich gifts.

Later, in the quiet of his rooms, King Solomon thought gratefully of the little bee which had served him so well. He humbly bowed his head. "I have been too proud," he thought. "None is so great that he needs no help, and none is so small that he cannot give it."

Surely, wisdom is given
to all living things,
And the tiniest creatures
are teachers of kings.

BENJAMIN ELKIN has been telling stories all his life, first to his own nine brothers and sisters, and then to the other children on the block in his native Baltimore. Now principal of the Rogers Elementary School in Chicago, Mr. Elkin is the author of more than a dozen books for children. Four of these have been chosen as Junior Literary Guild selections. He is the author of *Why the Sun Was Late* and *Such Is the Way of the World*, both published by Parents' Magazine Press.

ANITA LOBEL was born in Krakow, Poland. She attended school in Stockholm and later continued her studies at Washington Irving High School and Pratt Institute in New York City. She is the illustrator of *The Wishing Penny*, published by Parents' Magazine Press, and her distinctive art work for children can also be seen in *Puppy Summer* by Meindert De Jong. Mrs. Lobel is the wife of author-artist, Arnold Lobel, and the mother of two young children, Adrianne and Adam.